S0-AQL-752

Skip Count by 5, It's No Jive!

Tracy Kompelien

Consulting Editors, Diane Craig, M.A./Reading Specialist
and Susan Kosel, M.A. Education

Published by ABDO Publishing Company, 4940 Viking Drive, Edina, Minnesota 55435.

Printed in the United States.

Credits
Edited by: Pam Price
Curriculum Coordinator: Nancy Tuminelly
Cover and Interior Design and Production: Mighty Media
Photo Credits: ShutterStock, Wewerka Photography

Library of Congress Cataloging-in-Publication Data

Kompelien, Tracy, 1975-
    Skip count by 5, it's no jive! / Tracy Kompelien.
       p. cm. -- (Math made fun)
    ISBN 10 1-59928-543-6 (hardcover)
    ISBN 10 1-59928-544-4 (paperback)

    ISBN 13 978-1-59928-543-6 (hardcover)
    ISBN 13 978-1-59928-544-3 (paperback)
    1. Multiplication--Juvenile literature. 2. Counting--Juvenile literature. I. Title. II. Title: Skip count by five, it's no jive! III. Series.

    QA115.K6649 2007
    513.2'13--dc22

                                                    2006017373

SandCastle Level: Transitional

SandCastle™ books are created by a professional team of educators, reading specialists, and content developers around five essential components—phonemic awareness, phonics, vocabulary, text comprehension, and fluency—to assist young readers as they develop reading skills and strategies and increase their general knowledge. All books are written, reviewed, and leveled for guided reading, early reading intervention, and Accelerated Reader® programs for use in shared, guided, and independent reading and writing activities to support a balanced approach to literacy instruction. The SandCastle™ series has four levels that correspond to early literacy development. The levels help teachers and parents select appropriate books for young readers.

| **Emerging Readers** | **Beginning Readers** | **Transitional Readers** | **Fluent Readers** |
| (no flags) | (1 flag) | (2 flags) | (3 flags) |

These levels are meant only as a guide. All levels are subject to change.

To skip count by 5

is to count in groups of 5.

Words used
when skip counting:
fives
group
same

This is a group
of 5  .

5 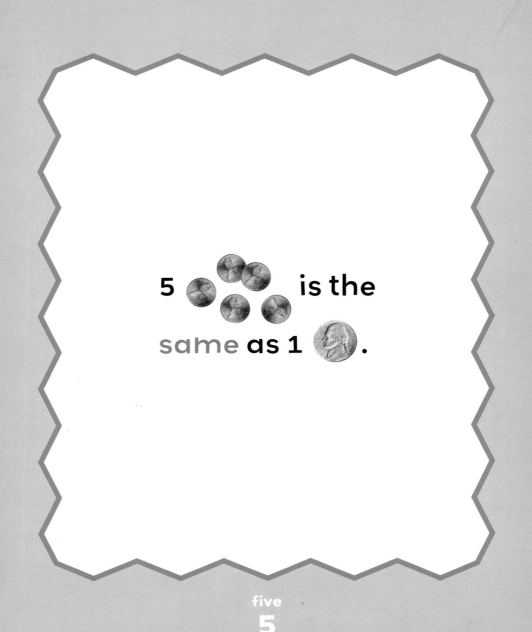 is the same as 1 .

On my there is a

group **of 5 toes.**

My  have two groups of 5 toes.

On my  there is

a group of 5 fingers.

On my ![hands] there are 2 groups of 5 fingers.

Skip Count by 5, It's No Jive!

Sally loves to tally!
She makes a note
as she counts
each vote.

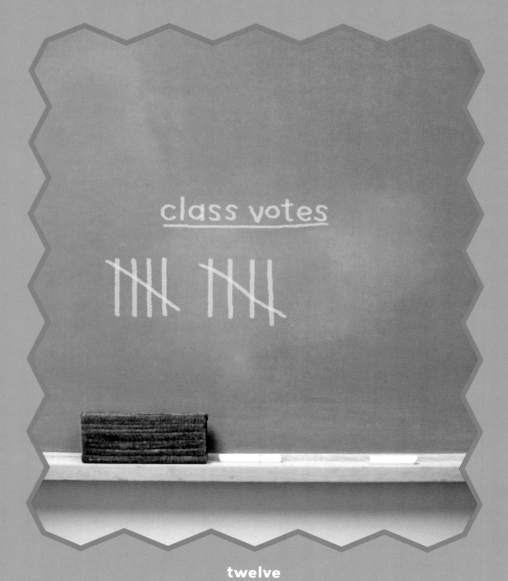

twelve

12

The correct answer will arrive when Sally **skip counts** by 5.

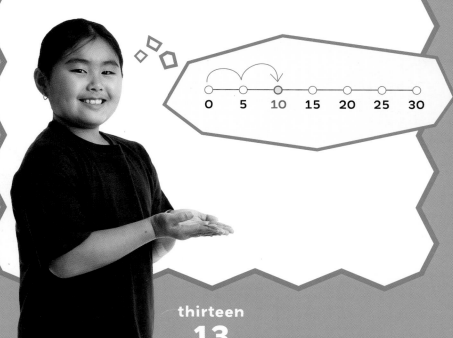

class votes

IIII IIII IIII

fourteen

14

Sally declares,

"It's no jive.

It is fun to

skip count by 5!"

0   5   10   15   20   25   30

fifteen
15

Skip Count by 5 Every Day!

To count my marble collection, I arrange the marbles into **groups** of 5.

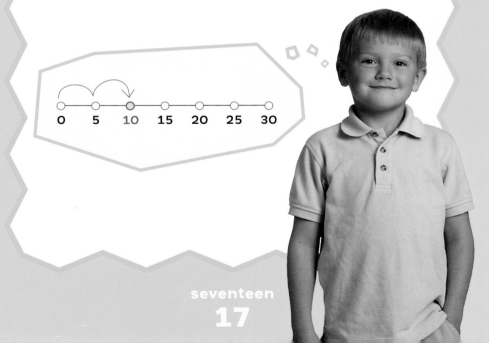

eighteen
18

The starfish have 5 points each. There are 6 starfish, which means there are 30 points.

twenty
20

I skip count my pencils in groups of 5.

Can you skip count by 5 to find how much money this is?

Each nickel is worth 5 cents, so this is 5, 10, 15, 20, 25, 30 cents!

Glossary

arrange – to put in a certain order.

group – a collection of things put together as a unit, especially things that have something in common.

jive – silly or foolish talk.

same – identical in every way.

tally – to keep count.